To Mai
Thanks for your support!

UNBOXED

Enjoy the book!

By Briana Morgan

Copyright © 2020 by Briana Morgan

All rights reserved. Except as permitted under the U.S. Copyright Act of 1976, no part of this publication may be reproduced, distributed, or transmitted in any form or by any means, or stored in a database or retrieval system, without the prior written permission of the author.

Briana Morgan
Atlanta, GA
Visit her website at www.brianamorganbooks.com

The characters and events portrayed in this book are fictitious. Any resemblance to real persons, living or dead, is coincidental and not intended by the author.

Book Cover by Johannus M. Steger
Edited by Coryl Addy
Paperback and Ebook Formatting by the Author
Blurb by Gemma Amor

To Gabe. Thank you for always believing in me, even when I don't believe in myself. I love you.

CHARACTERS

GREG ZIPPER	A man, 25-35 years old. Hosts a paranormal vlogging channel.
ALICE THORNE	A woman, 20-35 years old. An artist and Greg's girlfriend.
ROCCO	Greg and Alice's dog. Does not appear onstage.
THE BOXER	The person who sells Greg a dark web mystery box.
THE ENTITY	A dark, mysterious presence, summoned and controlled by the Boxer.

SETTING

The suburbs of a major metropolitan area. Autumn, over the span of several weeks.

ACT I

Scene 1: Greg and Alice's basement. Now.

Scene 2: The same basement. A few days later.

Scene 3: The basement. An hour later.

Scene 4: The basement. Several days later.

Scene 5: The park. About a half-hour later.

Scene 6: Greg and Alice's bedroom. Not long after the previous scene.

ACT II

Scene 1: Greg and Alice's kitchen. The next morning.

Scene 2: Outside Greg and Alice's house. Hours later.

Scene 3: Greg and Alice's basement. Several days later.

Scene 4: Greg and Alice's bedroom. Not long after the previous scene.

Scene 5: The park. Half an hour later.

Scene 6: Greg and Alice's basement. One week later.

ACT I

Scene 1

(Open on a basement set. There is a large computer desk with several monitors, a tower, and various technological equipment. An office chair sits in front of the desk, with a lamp, a television, and a couch off to one side. A washer and dryer can be seen, along with a staircase and a basement window in the background. The only wall art should be an award for GREG hitting 100K subscribers, along with a painting by ALICE. Any other furniture or decor can be left to the director's choice. GREG sits at the computer, firing up his platform and getting everything set up. He puts on a headset. There should be some way for the audience to see everything he is recording and broadcasting to the Internet.)

GREG: Okay, so… let me know if you guys can hear me okay. I'm turning off the chat because a few people got out of hand with it last time, but you can always hit me up on Twitter or whatever and let me know if this whole thing sucks. Wow, 700K. I can't believe we made it here. *(He pauses. Offstage, the sound of a door opening and the jingling of keys. GREG glances up toward the stairs, but doesn't seem too bothered by the noise.)* I was just going through comments from the Pinehurst Asylum video, and guys... holy shit, you picked up on things I didn't even notice. The shadow figure in the hallway–kudos to JasonX2002. I didn't even– (*Muffled talking noises from upstairs, and a dog barks several times. GREG winces, but the noise stops. His cell phone pings, he pulls it out of his pocket and checks it.*) Viper1910 wants to know if Alice and Rocco respect my filming schedule. Usually, the answer is yes, but this livestream was kind of spur of the moment, so... it's tricky, you know?

ALICE: (*Offstage.*) Greg, Rocco took a shit in the living room again! Can you come help me? I'm trying to put groceries away! (*GREG is visibly agitated, but he doesn't move. His phone pings a few times. ALICE tries again.*) Greg? I need you up here, please!

GREG: Not now, babe, I'm–I'm working on something! (*He checks his phone. Alice says something in response, but it is too muffled to hear. The audience is forced to ignore it, along with Greg. He reads from his phone notifications.*) NHD420 asks, "I've been a subscriber since the beginning. What's the coolest thing you've done thanks to Zipper Paranormal?" Yeeterman365, pretty much the same question. Um, that's a toughie! I've gotten to do so many cool things, but collaborating with the Doppler Twins and Leonardo Da Kitschy was beyond wicked. Those guys really know how to party. Who would've thought doing shots in a cemetery would draw out so many orbs? (*His phone pings again several times, in rapid succession. The dog starts barking again. ALICE yells, "Rocco!" The dog does not stop barking. We hear several things fall upstairs, the sound of breaking glass. GREG sets his phone down and drags his hand down his face.*) Alice, shut the damn dog up, please! (*His phone keeps pinging. ROCCO continues to bark. He tries to read from his phone instead, though the volume of the barking increases as he does so.*) TrentReznorsBiggestFan wants to know if I'm planning to check out the *Queen Mary* any time in the near– (*More glass breaks. ROCCO's barking hits a frenzied pitch.*) Alice!

ALICE: He's your damn dog too, Greg! Rocco, shut up! No, stay out of the living room, you've done enough–

GREG: Alice!

ALICE: For Christ's sake. (*She opens the door at the top of the stairs and yells down at GREG.*) You're the one who said you'd help me unload when I got back. That's what you agreed to. I can't do everything by myself.

GREG: (*Trying to keep his voice level.*) All I said was that I didn't want to go to the store with you. I never agreed to... anyway, I'm in the middle of streaming. (*He gestures toward his equipment.*)

ALICE: (*Coming down the stairs.*) You're streaming? Right now? Are you serious, Greg?

GREG: (*He gets up from the chair.*) Yeah, I'm streaming. You know, the thing I do that pays the bills? The thing that makes it possible for you to get your hair and nails done and pays for all your other bullshit? (*ROCCO starts barking again.*) And can you please, shut that goddamn dog up!

ALICE: All right, that's enough. Shut down the streaming. (*ROCCO keeps barking. ALICE goes to the computer and tries to turn it off. GREG intervenes.*) What are you doing?

GREG: What am I doing? What are you doing?

ALICE: I'm trying to turn this damn thing off.

GREG: Stop it. You're making it worse.

ALICE: How am I making it worse

GREG: Rocco, Jesus, please, stop barking! (*To ALICE.*) You're ruining this livestream.

ALICE: You're ruining it yourself, asshole.

GREG: Listen, don't be a bitch just because–

ALICE: What did you call me?

GREG: Okay, well, I didn't mean–

ALICE: Did you call me a bitch?

GREG: Alice, come on. We don't need to–

ALICE: Shut your mouth, Greg. I think we do. Rocco! (*He stops barking, abruptly. GREG's phone pings a few times and keeps pinging steadily throughout.*) Who the fuck is texting you?

GREG: Fan accounts! They're tuning in and probably wondering what the fuck is happening.

ALICE: Tell them to mind their own business.

GREG: It's my livestream. I think–

ALICE: You called me a bitch. Shut it down.

GREG: I don't want to.

ALICE: I don't care what you want. You can record something later. Right now, I need you to help with the dog.

GREG: I thought you wanted me to help with the groceries.

ALICE: Why does it have to be one or the other? Why can't it be both?

GREG: I can't fucking do everything!

ALICE: You don't do everything. You don't do much of anything, Greg. Not for the people who matter. (*She reaches past him and shuts off the screen.*)

UNBOXED

GREG: My subscribers don't matter? They're the ones who make all this possible, Alice. They bought us this house, your new car, the–

ALICE: I'd rather just have you than any of that shit. But they've taken you away from me, and you don't want to come back. (*Beat. GREG and ALICE stare pointedly at the red light blinking on the webcam.*)

GREG: Shit, it's still recording.

ALICE: I thought I turned it off.

GREG: You turned the screen off, not the webcam.

ALICE: (*Softly.*) You called me a bitch.

GREG: (*Working to shut off the webcam.*) I didn't mean it.

ALICE: Felt like you did.

GREG: I swear I didn't. I just got caught up in the moment is all.

ALICE: You've been living in that same moment for almost a year now.

GREG: I just hit 700,000 subscribers, Alice. That's not nothing. Can you blame me for being excited?

ALICE: I'm excited for you, okay? I helped you start the channel, for God's sake. I filmed for you, set up locations for you—

GREG: But you don't anymore.

ALICE: You *encouraged* me to work on my art. You said it was good for me

GREG: You were burning out, Alice.

ALICE: But I got to be with you. I got to spend more time with you, just the two of us. Behind the scenes.

GREG: *(Ignoring her.)* I wanted one livestream. One break from all the mundane shit. I didn't think that was too much to ask. *(He successfully shuts off the webcam and shuts down the computer. His phone pings again. GREG and ALICE both stare at it.)* I need to get that. It's the least I can do.

ALICE: Always going above and beyond for your fans. I wish…

GREG: *(Absentmindedly, while looking at his phone.)* What do you wish, Alice?

ALICE: I wish you'd pay attention to the people who really care about you, the ones that aren't a screen away. *(She heads back to the stairs, pausing at the bottom.)* Before it's too late. *(Alice goes back upstairs and shuts the door to the basement. GREG keeps scrolling through his phone. Lights fade.)*

ACT I

Scene 2

(*Lights up on the same basement set, a few days later. Nothing has changed, except for a pillow and mussed blankets on the couch, suggesting GREG has slept there. He sits at his desk scrolling around on the Internet while ALICE folds clothes and adds them to a basket near the dryer. Through the basement window, we can see it's raining. Thunder and rain sound effects throughout this scene.*)

ALICE: It's really coming down out there.

GREG: Yeah, I guess it is. That must be why the wi-fi's shitty.

ALICE: And why Rocco isn't down here with us right now.

GREG: Hopefully he's hiding and not shitting somewhere.

ALICE: Like you'd clean it up. (*Beat.*) I was thinking we could go to the movies this week. There's that new James Wan film, the one with the haunted carnival. It's getting good reviews.

GREG: Since when do you check reviews?

ALICE: You always ask about reviews before we see a movie. I thought I'd be proactive.

GREG: Yeah, maybe we could see that. (*He scrolls around and clicks on a few things before landing on another paranormal vlogger, perhaps one he knows or competes with. Muffled audio of the video plays through the computer speakers. GREG leans back from the screen.*) Hey... can I ask you something?

ALICE: Sure.

GREG: Do you watch any videos? Besides mine, I mean.

ALICE: Like... other vloggers?

GREG: Paranormal ones, specifically. (*He gestures toward the video.*) Take this one, for example. Terrified in Tokyo. This American dude who just moved to Japan started filming the weird shit that happened in his house, caught some of the most convincing footage in the community, and hit more than one million subs in less than a year. Know what his secret was?

ALICE: What?

GREG: This is the one that put him over the edge. It's a dark web mystery box unboxing.

ALICE: (*Pause.*) I understood none of those words.

GREG: You might if you still helped me with the channel. (*Repeating slowly.*) Dark web mystery box unboxing. It's... okay, give me a second. (*He pauses the video.*) The dark web is the seedy underbelly of the Internet. It's where all the fucked-up shit lives—drugs, sex trafficking, weapons... you name it, you got it. And everything is anonymous.

UNBOXED

ALICE: How does that work, though?

GREG: You use this open-source browser, Tor, to access everything. It's almost impossible to track someone through it. I mean, you'd have to be highly skilled to pull it off. Anyway, the way these videos work is that the person who owns the channel purchases a mystery box from a seller on the dark web, pays for it in Bitcoin—

ALICE: Bitcoin?

GREG: You know, like... cryptocurrency. Virtual money?

ALICE: Sure, Bitcoin.

GREG: After the box arrives, the person sets up their video camera and films the unboxing. Usually there's a bunch of fucked-up stuff inside, like baby teeth and bloody towels and human feces.

ALICE: Jesus.

GREG: But between you and me, most of it's fake. A lot of these channels—and this came directly from Leonardo Da Kitschy. When we did that collaboration, he said his publicist urged him to do one of the videos, offered to buy a bunch of thrift store shit and "make it look legit as possible." Leo turned him down, because he doesn't do anything paranormal-adjacent.

ALICE: Okay.

GREG: I'm not saying that's what Terrified in Tokyo did, but I guess I'm not saying he didn't do that either. I mean, there's no way of knowing for sure.

ALICE: (*She stops folding for a moment.*) You want to film one.

GREG: I didn't say that.

ALICE: You didn't *not* say it.

GREG: It could be the thing that puts me over the top. I could be Terrified in Tokyo.

ALICE: Except you want to do it legitimately, I'm guessing.

GREG: Well, yeah, of course. Otherwise, what's the point?

ALICE: It's dangerous, Greg. You said so yourself. Why can't you just fake one like everybody else? Hell, I could help you. I could run to the craft store, try my new paints —

GREG: I'm Zipper Paranormal. I don't fake anything.

ALICE: Just because you never have doesn't mean you couldn't.

GREG: Alice, when we started this channel, I said I wanted to only showcase genuine paranormal activity. "No cheesy pretend shit," remember?

ALICE: You also said you wouldn't do shit just because everyone else was doing it.

GREG: That was a long time ago, before I knew anything about trends and analytics. I've done some research, and I think my best shot at cracking one million subscribers is to go viral. Like, big-time, trending-page viral. And the best way I can think of to do that while still sticking with my niche is to do one of these dark web unboxing videos.

ALICE: But why do you have to buy a real box? There are so many unknowns with those.

GREG: Alice, my whole channel is *built* on unknowns.

ALICE: You said the dark web was dangerous. What if someone sends you a bomb or some shit? Something you can't walk away from.

GREG: I have to do something big to reach one million, Alice, otherwise I'll never make it.

ALICE: What are you talking about? You'll get there, babe. One million is only like, another 300K away. That's less than half of what you have now. Just keep chugging along and you'll hit it in no time.

GREG: I know I'll get there eventually, but... God, Terrified only had to wait a year to hit one mil. I've been trying for three years, and I don't want to wait three more. Hell, for all I know, the platform could go under. Paranormal videos might burn out, fade away. I could get demonetized. (*Beat.*) We could lose the car, the house. I mean, I have one strike now, and that scares the shit out of me. Two more and I'm out.

ALICE: Wait, since when did you get a strike? I thought you were fine.

GREG: I swear I told you about it.

ALICE: No way, I would've remembered something like that. I mean, I know you got a warning from that cemetery thing, when you were taking shots with those dudebros.

GREG: Leo and the twins are not dudebros... okay, maybe they are, but they're solid guys. Anyway, that wasn't a warning. That was my first strike. (*Pause.*) Apparently, more than a few people thought that we were being disrespectful.

ALICE: I told you not to do it.

GREG: It's not like we were the only ones to ever film a drinking game in a cemetery. How was I supposed to know?

ALICE: Wait, is that a thing? Other people have done that?

GREG: Yeah, where did you think I got the idea?

ALICE: Anyway.

GREG: Anyway, that was a strike. Two more and I'm out. I either get demonetized or banned, both of which spell disaster for the channel, and for my livelihood. So I guess what I'm saying is... the sooner I can hit one million, the better. It would more or less secure my spot, and it's harder for the platform to justify doing anything to me if I'm bringing that much engagement to them.

ALICE: That's assuming you don't film a dead body in a suicide forest or something.

GREG: Low blow, Alice. He apologized.

ALICE: Still was a shitty thing to do, if you ask me. Anyway, doesn't look like that's hurt him too badly. He's still pulling in ad revenue and shit, isn't he?

GREG: As far as I know. I think he still makes money from his channel. The thing is, if you get demonetized, you can't apply to get remonetized. Once you're out, you're out, and there's no coming back from it.

ALICE: It won't happen to you, Greg. You're careful.

GREG: Not careful enough. I just think I need to hit one million subscribers sooner rather than later.

ALICE: And you will, Greg. That's what I keep telling you. There's no need to film one of those unboxing videos—not for real, anyway. Please, for my sake, consider faking it? I'm more than willing to help. It could be good for us to work on this.

GREG: I can't fake it. I've built up trust with my fanbase. I can't give them any reason to doubt me.

ALICE: But this is the easiest way. Also, no one ever has to know you did this. I'm the only other person who knows, and I won't tell. What's there to worry about?

GREG: I'm not faking it, Alice. I don't care what happens. I can't do that to my fans. They trust me.

ALICE: Just because you fake one unboxing video doesn't mean you have to keep faking your content. You can stay genuine with the paranormal stuff. You just need a little boost to get you over the hump, right? So fake it. (*Pause.*) For my sake.

GREG: I don't know, Alice. I don't think it's the right move.

ALICE: Like I said, I can help you. I'll run out to the thrift store and grab a few things that would tell a strange story together. Mirrors and kids' backpacks. Miscellaneous shit. We'll figure it all out when I get back.

19

GREG: (*Hesitantly.*) What about Rocco? Does he need to go out?

ALICE: You can try to get him to go out in this weather, but I doubt he'll take the bait. Just set up for this video. (*She moves all the clothes to the hamper and heads up the stairs without another word. We hear her murmuring something, presumably to Rocco. Then, jingling keys, a door closing, a car starting and pulling away. Greg groans and goes back to working on the computer. He checks his camera set up, turns on the lighting, and starts filming himself. His tone changes drastically, as he is now using his "vlogger" voice.*)

GREG: What's up, all my ghosts and ghouls? Greg Zipper here with Zipper Paranormal. Today I have a special treat for you all. With the help of my lovely lady Alice Thorne, I've purchased a mystery box from the dark web, and I'm opening it live, just for all of you. Before I dive in, you might be wondering, what is a dark web mystery box? Basically, the dark web is a place where you can find the darkest shit, from drugs and hitmen to sex trafficking, and everything in between. The dark web— (*A violent flash of lighting and deafening thunder. Blackout. Rocco barks. Greg curses. End of scene.*)

ACT I

Scene 3

(Lights up on GREG's basement, illuminated by candles and flashlights. GREG works from his phone because there is no Internet connection on the laptop. His phone pings incessantly, and ROCCO can be heard barking faintly in the distance.)

GREG: Shit, shit, shit, shit, shit, shit, shit. *(Types a little bit, clicks on something, frowns.)* Fuck. Jesus Christ. *(Phone pings a few more times. He checks it.)* Shit. Goddamn it. Fuck! How the fuck did this happen? *(ALICE comes bounding down the stairs with two bags loaded with stuff from the local thrift store. She drops them on the couch and turns to GREG, smiling, oblivious to his frantic state. His phone does not stop pinging.)*

ALICE: They were having a tag sale today too, so I got so much shit for like nothing. It turned out to be—hey, what's going on? Who died?

GREG: My career, maybe.

ALICE: What do you mean?

GREG: You know how I was filming that livestream the other day? The spur-of-the-moment one you interrupted?

ALICE: (*Defensive.*) The one I had no way of knowing about?

GREG: Yeah. We had that disagreement—

ALICE: Fight.

GREG: Whatever it was. Well... it all got uploaded. Somehow.

ALICE: You mean, people can see it?

GREG: Yes, and they have. So many people. (*Alice goes over to stand beside him, watches for a minute as he scrolls through social media or his vlogging platform on his laptop. Then, she goes over to the wall switch and turns on the lights.*) Oh.

ALICE: (*As she goes around blowing out candles and turning off miscellaneous lanterns and flashlights.*) Stopped raining about an hour ago. How did it get uploaded?

GREG: Hell if I know. I got it taken down, but it looks like there are copies. Other people have uploaded it, and it keeps popping up.

ALICE: Can you petition the platform, make them stop the uploads?

GREG: Yeah, I just did. It can take a few days for them to respond though. Jesus. (*He is still clearly wound up.*) I'm trending on social media, and not in a good way.

ALICE: How much did they get?

GREG: Come on down and listen. (*He cues up the video. For this bit, it is not important to see the video, as long as the audience can clearly hear the audio from the argument in the first scene, including and especially the part where GREG calls ALICE a bitch.*)

ALICE: Oh my God.

GREG: I know.

ALICE: Why would anyone empathize with you?

GREG: I'm totally screwed now — what did you say?

ALICE: You sound like a total asshole right there. I still can't believe you called me a bitch just because I interrupted your video thing.

GREG: It was an important video thing. And Rocco was barking, and I asked you —

ALICE: Greg. I love you, but please. (*She goes over to the bag and starts taking items out of it without looking at GREG or responding to him. He watches her for a moment, shaking his head, clearly not pleased with what she's bought, although at this point, perhaps he knows better than to say so.*)

GREG: They're calling me a misogynist, saying I don't deserve you. I've already lost twenty thousand subscribers, and the number keeps dropping. I don't know what I — shit, there's the email from the platform. (*He pauses to read it to himself, and as he does so, his expression changes to shock.*) I'm... no, I just...

ALICE: (*Finally looking up.*) What is it?

GREG: I got another strike. One more, and I'm out.

ALICE: (*She stops unloading the bags.*) Wait, are you serious?

GREG: No word on whether they're taking care of the uploads. They just... they wanted me to know I violated their guidelines. Someone flagged it as abuse. (*Beat. They share a long, lingering look. GREG's face falls as he realizes, maybe for the first time, what a shitty boyfriend he's been.*) Alice, I'm... I didn't mean... Jesus, I'm sorry.

ALICE: I know, I know. (*Pause.*) Thank you. (*Her expression and tone soften as she goes back to unloading the bags.*) What are you going to do about this?

GREG: Um... well, I still have to wait to hear back about the uploads on the platform's end, but after that, I'll make an apology video, and maybe work with a freelance publicist. There has to be some way for me to recoup all my... what is it? Why are you staring at me?

ALICE: You stand to lose more than a couple subs, Greg.

GREG: (*Realization dawning.*) You weren't asking about the livestream.

ALICE: I don't understand what happened to us. We used to make everyone jealous. Even my mom said she'd never seen anything like us. I was so proud of you when you started this channel. It was so good for the both of us, something we could do together. It was such a slog, but hey, I got to be with you, and that was all I cared about. (*Pause.*) It meant something then. *I* meant something, Greg.

GREG: You still do.

ALICE: I don't think so. At least, I'm not convinced anymore. (*She gestures toward the empty bags and the stuff she's taken out of them.*) Anyway, here's your stuff. I think I'm going to lie down for a bit. Rocco should like that. I think he's been feeling neglected. (*She starts up the stairs.* GREG *looks over at the items without moving. She pauses to look at him, fighting tears. A sniffle or a cry escapes, and he turns his head, sharply, to look right at her.*)

GREG: (*He gets up and moves toward her. She doesn't move away from him.*) Alice. (*He takes her hand and looks at her.*) You still mean the world to me. I'm sorry, I just… I guess I don't know how I come across sometimes. How much I fuck up.

ALICE: I feel so isolated sometimes.

GREG: I know you do. I'm sorry. And I promise, I'm going to make it up to you, okay? Will you let me do that? (*She nods, and Greg pulls her down to kiss her on the forehead. She goes all the way up the stairs and through the door. He lets her.*) Shit, I've really stepped in it this time. (*He goes back down the stairs, shuts his laptop, picks up his phone, and scrolls through his phone for a minute, growing more and more dismal. He shuts the phone off and goes over to the couch to examine everything* ALICE *bought for his video. He studies a few objects and frowns, dissatisfied.*) Maybe this is a bad idea. Maybe… maybe the only way to be true to my word — to make up for being such an ass — is to hit the big time ASAP so I can spoil her. I shouldn't fake it after all. I need to do this thing for real. Sorry, Alice, but it's for the best. I'm going to make it up you, sooner than you think. (*He goes over to his camera and lighting setup and gets everything ready to film. Once again, he turns on his vlogger voice, puts his best face forward. As he addresses the camera, there is no trace of the broken, self-conscious man from earlier in the scene.* GREG *is truly in his* *element.*) Hey there, ghosts and ghouls. Today, I'm bringing you all a very special treat. Today... I'm going to order a dark web mystery box. (*He shuts off the camera, grabs a credit card, and rushes over to his computer. Blackout.*)

ACT I

Scene 4

(*Lights up on the basement again, several days later. From the light coming in through the basement window, we can tell it's early evening. There are still blankets and a pillow on the couch. GREG is working on the laptop when ALICE comes down the stairs, carrying a box. The box is taped up and unmarked, save for a FRAGILE stamp or sticker on the side of it, visible to the audience.*)

ALICE: Hey, Greg, what did you order? There's no address or anything.

GREG: (*Excitedly.*) Oh shit, that's the box!

ALICE: What box?

GREG: The dark web mystery box I ordered.

ALICE: (*Freezing.*) You ordered a box after I went out and bought all that thrift-store shit for you?

GREG: I thought I told you about it.

ALICE: I guess you thought wrong. (*She unceremoniously drops the box on the table and stands beside it with her hands on her hips.*) You owe me an apology.

GREG: Look, I appreciate you going out and getting all that stuff for me. I do. It's just...

ALICE: Not sounding much like an apology so far.

GREG: Well, I couldn't use that shit. None of it was good. I decided to make it authentic, do the real thing. (*Pause.*) For us.

ALICE: You mean, that thing I suggested you do in the first place? Not fake the unboxing?

GREG: Yeah. I mean, I guess so.

ALICE: You guess so?

GREG: Can we not do this?

ALICE: Yeah, I don't know why I even bother anymore. I'm going to take Rocco out for a walk. In the meantime, feel free to turn the asshole down a notch. (*She stomps upstairs and slams the door again. A moment later, we hear jingling keys, and another door opens and closes.*)

GREG: Christ alive. (*He stares at the box for a few minutes before going over to his desk and pulling gloves and a knife out of the drawer. He repositions his camera and his lighting so that they're facing the box and the contents of the box. GREG eyes the pillows and blankets on the couch and hastily moves them out of the way. He puts on a hat that says ZIPPER on it and sits on the couch. He pulls the box on his lap, puts the gloves on and picks up the knife. Then, he realizes the camera isn't recording.*) Shit. (*He sets the box* *aside, goes over to the camera, and hits record. He sits back down on the couch and picks up the box again. We see his expression change from one of dismay and annoyance to one of delight, almost wonder. His energy is up as he speaks.*) Good morning, ghosts and ghouls! So... this arrived in the mail for me today. No labels, no address, no anything—well, except for this sticker or whatever that says FRAGILE. You can guarantee that one was ignored. Hopefully, there's still something salvageable here. (*He takes the knife and cuts the tape on the box as he speaks.*) As you can see, I'm wearing gloves, because you never know what shit you'll find in these things. I've watched other videos where people have found guns, bloody fabric, and even syringes. Totally not taking any chances on this. If shit goes sideways, I'd rather not get my fingerprints on something I plan to turn in to the police. God willing, I won't even have to worry about that though. (*He sets the knife aside and peers into the box. The audience cannot see what's inside.*) Dude. Holy shit. (*He sticks his hand inside, winces, swears, and jerks it back out. He's bleeding from a cut in his palm.*) Fuck. What the hell? (*GREG looks into the box again.*) Jesus, it looks like there's some broken glass in here. Give me a second. (*He takes out a shattered bottle.*) That's what I thought. Something fragile, unprotected. Perfect for slicing up Zipper's soft skin. Let's see what else we have in here. (*GREG pulls out a card. He reads it aloud to the camera.*) "I am the shadow in the dark. I am the whisper in the night. I am your worst nightmare. I am the Boxer." (*GREG rolls his eyes.*) Melodramatic much? Jesus. I guess that's the guy who put this thing together. Boxer, if you're watching, you seem pretty lame. Hope you're laughing as you swim in all that Bitcoin I sent you. Nice ploy there, dude. (*He rummages around in the box and pulls out an old baby doll, which he sets beside the note and the broken bottle.*) Nice. (*He goes in again and takes out a pile of hair.*) This looks like human hair. That's gnarly. (*He sets the hair on the table, takes out a box of matches. He opens the box, lights a match, and shows it to the camera before blowing it out and setting the matches aside. Lastly, he takes out a bleached animal skull, seemingly from a small rodent or dog.*) Okay, what the hell? Is that really all there is? (*He shakes the box a little. The glass rattles around inside. As he looks back at the table, his gaze falls on the baby doll again, and he frowns.*) Hang on a minute. (*GREG twists the baby doll head, and it pops off. He digs around inside the severed head and pulls out a note, which he accidentally smears some blood on.*) Shit. (*He unfolds the note and reads it out loud, frowning.*) "You are the hapless. You are the weak. You are the summoner. You are my link. With blood from your hands, the Entity rises. Careful now, Zipper. Here come the surprises." (*GREG pales.*) What the fuck? He knows my name? It's supposed to be anonymous. (*He reads the note again, hands shaking somewhat. Then, he sets the note aside and shoves everything back in the box. He shuts off the camera, takes off his gloves, and tosses them into the trash. He goes upstairs. A minute later, he comes back down, pressing a dish towel against his bleeding hand.*) How the fuck does he know my name? Maybe it's a fan just messing with me. Or hell, it's Alice. That makes more sense. (*He winces at the pain in his hand again and readjusts the towel. A door opens upstairs, with jingling keys and the sound of a dog scuffling around. Greg looks up and yells up the stairs.*) Alice, could you come down here please? I want to show you something.

ALICE: Give me just a second. (*We hear her take off Rocco's leash, and Rocco takes off running to another part of the house. Once she has handled the dog, ALICE comes part of the way down the stairs.*) Hey, what's up? What's wrong with your hand?

GREG: Did you do this?

ALICE: Do what?

GREG: Set up this box. Send it to me, or whatever. Is this some kind of joke?

ALICE: I don't know what you're talking about. I went out and got all that shit for you, that's it. Whatever you did after that, I had nothing to do with it, nothing.

GREG: I cut my fucking hand on a broken lightbulb, Alice.

ALICE: How is that my fault?

GREG: I'm just saying, it seems pretty convenient that we get into some fights, this package shows up, the Boxer mentions me by name, and —

ALICE: He mentioned you by name? I thought it was anonymous.

GREG: Yeah, so did I. You see why I'm suspicious?

ALICE: Who's the Boxer?

GREG: The guy who put this thing together.

ALICE: He left you a note?

GREG: Two notes.

ALICE: Let me see one.

GREG: Hang on. (*He goes over to the things he's pulled out of the box and gingerly plucks the Boxer's note from the pile, not the one about the Entity. He hands it to ALICE.*) It doesn't look like your handwriting, but I still wasn't sure.

ALICE: I said I didn't do it. (*She takes the note from him and reads it aloud once again.*) "I am the shadow in the dark. I am the whisper in the night. I am your worst nightmare. I am the Boxer." What the fuck does that mean? You thought I would write this?

GREG: I don't know what I thought.

ALICE: Well, that's what you said, Greg. You thought it was me.

GREG: It doesn't sound like you, okay? You're right. I shouldn't have accused you.

ALICE: (*She eyes his hand.*) Do you think you need stitches? We should go to the hospital.

GREG: I don't think it's deep; it just bled a lot. That glass was sharp. This Boxer dude... I don't know. He seems like an asshole.

ALICE: Takes one to know one, I suppose. (*Beat. The two of them speak at the same time.*)

GREG: Look, I wanted —

ALICE: I was hoping — (*Pause.*)

GREG: You first.

ALICE: I was going to say, I was hoping we could get out for a little while, just the two of us. We haven't had a date night in a long time, and I think it would do us some good.

GREG: I think so, too. I wanted to say I'm sorry... for everything lately. I've been an asshole.

UNBOXED

ALICE: Yeah, you have.

GREG: Anyway, I want to make it up to you. That is, if you'll let me.

ALICE: I think I'll let you. (*She looks at his hand.*) First, I think maybe I should take a look at that.

GREG: Sure thing. (*He starts up the stairs. ALICE glances over at the box.*)

ALICE: How'd it go, by the way? The unboxing?

GREG: It... might have been a bust. I guess we'll wait and see. (*GREG rethinks something and heads back down the stairs. He sets up the camera again as ALICE watches, hands on her hips. He hits RECORD, and the red light flashes. Satisfied, he steps away from the camera and moves toward ALICE. The two of them head upstairs. The door closes. Enter the ENTITY, in the form of a silhouette, if possible. GREG's desk lamp flickers, and a painting drops off the wall. Lights fade.*)

ACT I

Scene 5

(*Lights up on a park, a drastic change from GREG's basement. There is a park bench, trees, a fountain, shrubbery, etc. All is lit by a street lamp or two, soft and romantic. The bubbling of a fountain and the chattering of insects underscores the scene as it unfolds. GREG and ALICE sit on a picnic blanket next to a basket. GREG opens it up, takes out a bottle of wine and two glasses, along with bread and cheese. He uncorks the wine, wincing at the pain in his hand, and pours a little for both of them as he speaks.*)

GREG: Long time since we've been here.

ALICE: Our first date. I thought you'd forgotten.

GREG: Never. You were wearing that short black dress... way too formal for the park, and it made sitting difficult, but damn if you didn't wear it like you were doing it a favor.

ALICE: (*Taking a glass of wine from him.*) Meanwhile, you were wearing a Star Wars shirt and jeans. (*Pause.*) You always know how to make a girl feel special.

GREG: Even assholes still have a few tricks up their sleeve.

ALICE: What, no candles?

GREG: Fire hazard. Besides, we'll make our own ambiance.

ALICE: (*Raising her glass.*) Let's toast, okay?

GREG: To what?

ALICE: To us, maybe. To the good old days, and all the new ones left to come.

GREG: To Greg Zipper and Alice Thorne, modern-day legends. (*They clink their glasses and drink. Both are quiet for a moment. GREG stares into his glass, reflecting.*) Is our life anything like what you thought it would be?

ALICE: (*Pause.*) Your channel blowing up, all the ad money, the house, the dog, the fancy trips... I never expected any of that. My life has changed so much, and all because of you.

GREG: Well, it's been my pleasure.

ALICE: I would have been happy without any of it, Greg. All I've cared about, since the very beginning, is you. It's us. That's all that really matters.

GREG: But... surely you don't regret me making the channel? Look how far it's gotten us.

ALICE: How far it's gotten you. (*Pause.*) Don't get me wrong, I'm thankful for all that we have, and even more thankful to have all of it plus you. It's just... sometimes I miss how we were in the beginning. Grilled cheese on a dorm room hot plate, stealing silverware from the cafe, movie nights on the quad where we'd sneak in rum and Cokes.

GREG: Sounds like you miss college.

ALICE: No, Greg. I miss us. I miss when life was simpler. You used to look at me like I was the only thing in the world that mattered to you. Now, I catch you giving that same look to your computer.

GREG: Don't try to blame it on the platform again. It gave us everything.

ALICE: I know that. I just wish it hadn't taken it all, too.

GREG: (*He pours himself another glass of wine and reaches for ALICE's. She gives it to him, and he tops hers off too.*) I'm going to be better about making time for you. About making time for us. I promise you, Alice.

ALICE: I've never asked for much.

GREG: And you deserve it all. Everything I've done, everything I've earned us... I'd give you a castle on the beach if I could, a diamond tiara.

ALICE: Let's start with a ring, huh?

GREG: Does that mean I'm forgiven?

ALICE: You haven't fully apologized yet.

GREG: You're right. I'm sorry. (*He scoots closer to her, and his tone softens. This is a sincere GREG, the likes of which we haven't yet witnessed. This is a man afraid of losing what he loves, who only just now realizes how close he's come to that. Maybe he even takes* *her hand as he speaks.*) I'm sorry for being a class-action jackass. I'm sorry for yelling and cursing at you. None of what happened is what you deserve, and none of it's your fault. I lost sight of us, is all. I mean, that's no excuse, but I... Jesus, Alice. I want to do better. Will you let me try again? Will you stay with me, please?

ALICE: (*Bantering.*) You'd never make it on your own. Of course I'll stay with you. (*They kiss. When they pull apart, ALICE rests her forehead against GREG's.*) You think it will be easier for us from now on?

GREG: That's what I'm hoping. It's what I've been working toward. After what I filmed earlier, I think I'm finally on the right track. And I promise, I will be less of a dick.

ALICE: That's what I like to hear.

GREG: I'm going to make it up to you, Alice. I promise. I don't want you ever questioning whether you're better off without me, because I'll do everything in my power to provide for you, make sure you never want to be without me.

ALICE: Greg, I just want you. That's all that matters to me. If you can promise me that—your full attention, your devotion, your love... everything else is just a bonus.

GREG: And that's what I like to hear. (*He kisses her again, longer and more passionately. This time, when they break apart, both of them are smiling.*) You, uh, want to get out of here?

ALICE: I thought you'd never ask. (*They gather up the picnic, the wine, and the glasses. Lights fade.*)

ACT I

Scene 6

(*Lights up on GREG and ALICE's bedroom, with both of them in pajamas and ready for sleep for the evening. GREG sits with his laptop propped on his lap and a dog-shaped bundle under the covers at his feet. ALICE sits near him, reading a book. The only light comes from a bedside lamp. Any other furnishings in the room are open to negotiation, as they are not immediately relevant to the events that unfold. GREG's hand is still bandaged up from where the broken bottle cut him.*)

GREG: I'm definitely not getting demonetized anytime soon. Seven hundred thousand views and climbing.

ALICE: What about subscribers?

GREG: Not quite as many as I'd like, but I just passed 600K again. They're all coming back, for the most part.

ALICE: Still on track to hit one mil?

GREG: Yeah. I think so, anyway. I guess we'll find out soon. You know... I don't ever think I thanked you for the painting thing?

ALICE: (*Without looking up from her book.*) What painting thing? *My* painting?

GREG: When we got back from the park last night, I mean, hours later... I took a look at the footage from the camera in the basement—

ALICE: You set up a camera in the basement?

GREG: I was hoping for something exciting, not really expecting anything, but you know how paranormal shit goes. I wanted to be ready for anything.

ALICE: How much did it cost?

GREG: Don't worry about it. Anyway, I'm trying to express my gratitude here, if you'd give me a chance.

ALICE: Gratitude for what? I'm not following.

GREG: The painting. Or rather, what happened with the painting. Not too long after I opened the box. (*He pauses long enough for ALICE to sense he's waiting for her to get it. She sets down her book and levels her gaze at him.*) You still don't know what I'm talking about?

ALICE: No, Greg, I don't.

GREG: Right when we left, a painting fell off the wall. And the lights flickered, but that's not as convincing. I don't know how you got the painting to fall, but it looked so damn good.

Gave me the chills. The flickering is easy enough to debunk, if anyone really wanted to, but still a good effort.

ALICE: I didn't touch the painting. I was with you.

GREG: No, yeah, I know that. You set it up before we left, somehow without me knowing. And whatever you did with the lamp was pretty clever too.

ALICE: I don't know what you're talking about. I didn't do anything to the lamp.

GREG: You can cut the act. It's just us. No cameras in here, though if I had my way…

ALICE: Come on, Greg. I'm serious.

GREG: What do you mean?

ALICE: I didn't touch any of your stuff in the basement. I never interfere unless you ask me to. You should know that by now.

GREG: Wait, are you serious?

ALICE: Yes! I just told you… (*She registers the panic and confusion on his face.*) Hang on, are you serious?

GREG: It's not funny anymore.

ALICE: I know it's not. Neither of us is joking now, right?

GREG: Right.

ALICE: So… what does that mean?

GREG: You know how I always say, "If logic can't explain it, it's likely paranormal?"

ALICE: Well, maybe it had something to do with the house settling. Maybe Rocco ran into a wall. Or... or maybe when we closed the door upstairs, we —

GREG: But what about the flickering light?

ALICE: Loose connection. Faulty wiring.

GREG: It worked just fine before. (*Silence stretches between them. The bundle at Greg's feet shifts. ALICE stretches to pet it.*)

ALICE: What all was in the box, Greg? You said there were notes, plural. What did the rest say?

GREG: Well, there was the main one, the riddle or whatever from the person who put it together.

ALICE: Right.

GREG: And the other one... uh, I didn't really want to bother you with it. Kinda fucked up, now that I think about it. That's the one where the Boxer mentions my name.

ALICE: Zipper Paranormal? That's your public handle.

GREG: Just the last name, Zipper. And yes, it's public, but when you buy something on the dark web... like I said, it's supposed to be anonymous. Not impossible to trace, but pretty fucking tough.

ALICE: What did the note say, Greg? (*GREG sighs and clicks around on the laptop. He pulls up his unboxing video and skips around until he gets to the part with the note about the ENTITY.*)

ALICE *scoots closer to watch. We hear the audio from the video play as GREG reads the note onscreen.)*

GREG (V.O.): "You are the hapless. You are the weak. You are the summoner. You are my link. With blood from your hands, the Entity rises. Careful now, Zipper. Here come the surprises."

GREG: *(He pauses the video and looks pointedly at ALICE, who shakes her head.)* I know you didn't write that. We've established that much. And you didn't do the other shit in the basement, the shit that got recorded after we left. There's only one other explanation.

ALICE: Someone else is fucking with you.

GREG: What? No, it's ghosts.

ALICE: Greg, this person knows your name. Maybe it's someone who doesn't like you. Somehow, they figured out who you are, and now they're trying to scare you.

GREG: You saw all the paranormal shit.

ALICE: No, what I saw was a flickering light and a painting falling off the wall. It could've been anything.

GREG: We already ruled out—

ALICE: We didn't rule out anything. I gave you some perfectly logical excuses for what happened, and you shot me down. That doesn't prove it's paranormal. It just proves you're an asshole, which we already knew.

GREG: I can do without the snark, thanks.

ALICE: Likewise.

GREG: Maybe it's both.

ALICE: What is?

GREG: Maybe someone's messing with me, and it's paranormal. (*Beat.*) Think about it. The note about the Entity or whatever the fuck it is said something about blood. And I cut my hand to all hell on those glass shards, smeared my blood on the paper...

ALICE: You think somebody cursed you? Like, you unleashed a spell or something?

GREG: I don't know. It's possible.

ALICE: I just wish you'd done more research before getting into this.

GREG: How was I supposed to know some freaky shit would happen?

ALICE: You're the king of freaky shit. It's what your whole channel is based on, remember?

GREG: I need to look through the box again, make sure I'm not missing something. When I cut my hand on the glass, it derailed the whole thing. I was distracted—something could've slipped by without me noticing.

ALICE: You're usually so thorough, I don't know how that would have happened.

GREG: Yeah, I'll be right back. (*GREG gets out of the bed and leaves the room to fetch the box. ALICE debates grabbing GREG's* *laptop and snooping a little, but settles for going back to her book until GREG returns with the box in tow.) Found it. (He sits on the bed and opens the box.)*

ALICE: Careful.

GREG: It's okay now. I dumped out all the glass. *(He rummages through the box, pulling out the now-familiar items one by one: both notes including the bloodstained one, the decapitated baby doll, the hair, the matches, and the animal skull. ALICE takes the baby doll head and turns it this way and that, studying it intently. GREG opens the box of matches again, and pulls out a small slip of paper he missed when he first opened the box. With some ceremony, he unfolds the paper.)* It's an address. A P.O. box.

ALICE: Why would they send that?

GREG: It says something here... let me turn the light up. *(He runs over to the wall and flips a switch, flooding the room with overhead lighting. Carefully, he reads the note.)* "All gods demand some form of tribute. Send an offering here, and try to earn my favor." *(Pause.)* This one doesn't rhyme. Guess he got tired of being clever.

ALICE: What "tribute" do you think he's talking about?

GREG: *(Looking back at the box.)* Human hair, maybe. Some kind of sacrifice?

ALICE: Sacrifice? Jesus. What about money?

GREG: I already sent him a shit ton of money. This box set me back like... an obscene amount.

ALICE: You don't want to tell me how much it cost, do you?

GREG: It was all ad money. No living expenses. I promise you, Alice. We're totally fine. I'd never jeopardize our living situation.

ALICE: Well, whatever's going on, there might be something in our house. So... you'll have to forgive me if I don't trust that promise.

GREG: If anything, it's just a ghost. Not like... a demon.

ALICE: How do you know that?

GREG: (*He sighs.*) Yeah... I'll work on it. First thing tomorrow morning.

ALICE: You'd better.

GREG: (*He puts everything back in the box and takes the baby doll head from ALICE. After setting the box on the floor beside the bed, he turns off the overhead light. He climbs back into bed, and ALICE shuts off the light. They kiss.*) Goodnight, Alice.

ALICE: Goodnight, Greg. Love you.

GREG: You too. (*Silence. For a minute, it seems like the scene has ended, but there is a creak in the hallway. ROCCO whines.*) Go to sleep, boy. It's nothing. (*Another creak, the sound of keys jingling as they fall off the rack. ROCCO growls.*) Shit. Alice, turn on the light.

ALICE: (*She does, sitting up against the pillows, while GREG sits bolt upright, clutching the blankets.*) Aren't you going out there to see what it is? (*ROCCO growls again. ALICE reaches down to pet him. The lamp flickers, and ROCCO barks. GREG swings his legs over the side of the bed. He opens the nightstand drawer and pulls out a pistol.*) Hang on, what the fuck is that?

GREG: What does it look like?

ALICE: How long have you had that? You know I hate guns.

GREG: I really don't think now's the best time for this. (*He turns the safety off and rummages in the drawer. More noises are heard from outside the bedroom. ROCCO whines some more.*)

ALICE: Greg, just go out there!

GREG: I'm looking for bullets.

ALICE: Jesus fucking Christ, just give it up and go.

GREG: I got one. (*He loads a bullet into the chamber and cocks the gun. The lights flicker again. GREG prepares to go out into the hallway, lingering by the door. Then, there's the jingling of a dog collar, and through the crack in the door, we see a dog's silhouette. GREG lowers the gun in shock.*) Oh my God. Alice— (*He turns toward her just as she reaches for the lump in the bed. The light bulbs in the house shatter. ALICE screams. The real ROCCO in the hallway barks, and a deep, demonic laugh echoes through the house. GREG grabs a flashlight and switches it on. He points it at the bed, where ALICE cowers in terror. There is no lump under the covers.*) Alice. A-Alice... did you see Rocco get under the covers? Did you actually—

ALICE: N-no, I didn't. He was, I mean, when we got into bed, he was already—

(*A sonic boom shakes the house. GREG drops the flashlight and runs into the hallway, still wielding the gun. He fires it. ALICE cries. Blackout. End of act. Intermission to follow.*)

ACT II

Scene 1

(*Lights up on GREG and ALICE's kitchen. A bullet hole and spider-webbed cracks mar the window over the sink, and another one appears on a cabinet door. Shattered glass lines the counter and sink. A weary-looking GREG and ALICE sit at the kitchen table, nursing cups of coffee. The dark web mystery box sits in the middle of the table with the contents still inside. ROCCO's distant barking echoes from the backyard. For a while, the only other sound is the ticking of the clock.*)

GREG: (*He stares down into his coffee cup as he speaks, as though he's afraid to meet ALICE's gaze.*) I talked to the window guy first thing this morning. They'll have to replace the whole pane of glass. I haven't called about the cabinet yet, but you've never liked the style, anyway.

ALICE: (*She sips her coffee and looks past GREG to the window.*) You could've hit Rocco. You know that, right?

GREG: Yeah, I could have, but I didn't. You saw him. He's fine.

ALICE: No one here's fine. Not after last night.

GREG: I'll get rid of the gun.

ALICE: It's not about that. Not entirely. You know what I'm saying.

GREG: I'm sending him money once I've finished my coffee.

ALICE: The Boxer? As tribute?

GREG: I don't know what else to do here. Neither of us got any sleep last night, right? You want to spend another night like that tonight? How about the night after? It's worth a shot. Besides, I don't have anything else to offer him besides more money.

ALICE: What if you reached out to that exorcist? You know, Father Normandy? I think that was his name. You interviewed him for that special like a year ago or something. Maybe he could help us.

GREG: I don't think it's a demon.

ALICE: Well, we don't know what it is. Father Normandy might be able to tell.

GREG: I'll send the Boxer some more money first, and we'll see what happens.

ALICE: You could do both. Send him the money, then reach out to the Father.

GREG: Yeah, I guess. It just feels dumb.

ALICE: You shot two holes in our kitchen last night. There was something in our bed. Not acting is dumb.

GREG: I wish I'd never ordered the box in the first place.

ALICE: Me too. But we can't unring that bell. We have to move forward.

GREG: I'll go get my wallet. (*He gets up from the table and heads into the other room. ALICE gets up from her seat and goes over to the window. She presses her hand to the cracked glass, frowning. Then, she goes over to the cabinet with the hole in it, opens it up, and takes out some shattered mugs. GREG returns and stops when he notices her.*) Did I fuck up something else?

ALICE: The first mug I got you. The one I made in my college ceramics class. (*She holds a broken piece of it up for his inspection. He steps close to her, takes it from her hand, and sets it on the counter. He slips his hand into hers.*)

GREG: Careful there, babe. You'll cut yourself. (*Suddenly, ALICE throws her arms around his neck and buries her face in his shoulder. It takes GREG a minute to put his arms around her and reciprocate the embrace. The two of them stand there for a moment in silence, just holding each other. ALICE sniffles, but only cries softly. The only other indication that she has been crying is that, when they pull apart, she wipes at her eyes. GREG touches her face, maybe even tucks her hair behind her ears.*) Alice, I'm so sorry. I love you.

ALICE: I'm scared.

GREG: So am I, but we can do this. We can get through it together. Not long from now, this will all just be a distant nightmare. I'm going to fix this. I promise you that.

ALICE: I know you will. Thank you. *(He kisses her forehead and goes back to the table, armed with his wallet. ALICE follows him, sits back down in front of her coffee, and sips it with trembling hands.)*

GREG: Once everything is over, we should take a trip somewhere. We haven't really taken a vacation in a while. You, me, maybe Rocco. It'll do us some good.

ALICE: We can go to the beach. Get sunburned and everything.

GREG: Sand in our crotches. Dirty band-aids floating by. Kids shitting in tide pools.

ALICE: *(Teasing, as she smiles.)* Don't be so gross.

GREG: Oh, come on. You know you love it.

ALICE: I do, but you should stop now, before I lose interest.

GREG: In me, or the beach?

ALICE: Both. *(GREG takes a wad of cash out of his wallet. ALICE whistles as he thumbs through the bills before folding them together and sliding them into an envelope. He writes the address on the front, grabs a stamp from the drawer, and licks the envelope to seal it closed before slapping a stamp on it. ALICE finishes her coffee and stands with her empty cup. She collects GREG's as she passes and takes both of them over to the sink. Then, she leans against the counter, watching GREG for a minute as he examines the contents of the box once again.)* You really think this will fix everything? Get the Boxer off our back, call off the Entity?

GREG: I don't know, really. But it can't make things worse. *(He holds up the envelope. She nods. Then, he sticks it in his pocket* *and heads for the front door.*) Hey, here's an idea: let's get out of the house again. Go somewhere fun.

ALICE: We could take Rocco to the park.

GREG: No, just you and me.

ALICE: (*Reluctantly.*) I don't know. I don't want to leave Rocco home alone right now.

GREG: The Boxer didn't leave me any weird notes about dogs.

ALICE: I just have a weird feeling.

GREG: It'll be all right, I promise. He's a big dog, and we won't be gone long.

ALICE: Maybe you're right. (*Relenting.*) We could go to the movies, see that James Wan flick.

GREG: Yeah.

ALICE: I'll even let you buy me popcorn.

GREG: Hell yeah. It's a date. (*He winks and heads outside to take the letter to the mailbox. ALICE goes to wash the cups, sees something in the corner of the kitchen, and freezes. Puzzled, she reaches for the object, grabs it, and pulls it out. It's a small camera with wires attached and a blinking light on top.*)

ALICE: What the fuck? (*GREG returns as she continues to examine it. She holds it up to show him.*) Did you put this up?

GREG: What is it?

ALICE: What does it look like?

GREG: What the fuck?

ALICE: That's what I said.

GREG: Okay, let me take a look. (*He takes the camera from ALICE and smashes it against the counter until the screen breaks and the light stops blinking. Parts go everywhere.*)

ALICE: Jesus.

GREG: I bet this is the Boxer. I don't know how, but I think... somehow, he got in here. It might have even been him in here last night.

ALICE: I thought it was a ghost or something. And what was in our bed?

GREG: I don't know. Maybe... maybe we should get out of here for a while.

ALICE: Call the police first. Maybe they can do a sweep while we're out of the house.

GREG: I don't know if that's a good idea. These dark web mystery boxes... this shit is illegal. If we get them involved, I don't know what could happen.

ALICE: Are you kidding me right now? Our lives could be in danger. I don't think they'll arrest you when we're being threatened by something.

GREG: I mean... I guess you're right. We have plenty of other shit to worry about here. (*Pause. ROCCO barks outside. Both of them look toward the window.*) Tell you what. I'll go bring Rocco in, both of us can change, and we'll go see that movie. How does that sound?

ALICE: Call the police first, and you've got a deal. (*GREG takes out his cell phone and dials the police ALICE goes into the other room. GREG opens the door to the outside.*)

GREG: Hi, yeah, I'd like to report a crime. Well, maybe the intent for a crime. My address? Sure, it's... (*GREG's voice fades, as do the lights, as he closes the door behind him.*)

ACT II

Scene 2

(*Lights up on the exterior of GREG and ALICE's house. The front door is painted red, but all other details are left to the whims of the stage manager and/or scenic designer, save one: an innocent-looking box rests on the front steps, waiting to be discovered. A note sits on top of the box, weighted down by a rock. GREG and ALICE enter from offstage, chatting and laughing about the movie. GREG is the first to notice the box on the steps. He freezes. The air is still, with no other sounds in the background; no crickets, cicadas, lawn mowers, sprinklers... no neighborhood noise. It's as though the atmosphere itself knows something bad is coming. ALICE doesn't notice he's stopped and runs right into him.*)

ALICE: Greg? What's — (*She looks past him to the box sitting on the front porch and covers her mouth with her hand.*) Did you... order something?

GREG: No way. Did you? (*ALICE shakes her head. GREG is visibly anxious. He holds a hand out to deter ALICE from moving forward.*) Stay here.

ALICE: When you called the cops earlier, what did they say?

GREG: They can't do anything without real evidence, some proof of a tangible threat. Dial 911 just in case, but don't press the button. Not yet, anyway.

ALICE: Greg.

GREG: I know, be careful. I'll take it real slow. (*ALICE dials the number. GREG creeps toward the box with clear trepidation. He crouches down in front of the box, picks up the rock, and reads the note, hands trembling as he does so.*) "You're a dick, Greg, but that's not the worst part. You're a dick with money, and you think that means you matter. That wasn't the offering I wanted from you. All you self-important vloggers think the world revolves around you, that you can make all your problems disappear with a snap of your fingers and a wave of some cash. Well, I'm good at making things disappear, too. And reappear elsewhere. Open the box."

ALICE: Greg, I don't think... what if it's a bomb?

GREG: That's not his style. (*He swallows and slowly opens the box, which hasn't been sealed. He looks inside, and confusion dawns on his face, followed quickly by horror. He drops the box and staggers backward.*)

ALICE: Greg? What is it? What's in the box?

GREG: I-I c-can't, Alice, it's... it just... (*He shakes all over as he reaches into the box and lifts out a bloodstained dog collar with a tag that reads ROCCO. ALICE's phone falls from her hand as she shrieks and runs toward him. He tries to stop her from opening the front door, but fails. She rushes inside. GREG drops the collar and vomits into the bushes. Inside the house, ALICE screams. Lights fade.*)

ACT II

Scene 3

(*Lights up on the basement, several days after the events of the previous scene. Same setup as usual. ALICE and GREG sit on the couch. There is a tissue box on the table in front of them, and several crumpled tissues between them. ALICE holds ROCCO's collar like it's a lifeline. It's clear both ALICE and GREG have been crying. GREG is on his laptop. There is a book on the table in front of ALICE, but she doesn't interact with it. Mostly, she stares straight ahead, zoned out. GREG's cell phone rests on the table in front of him.*)

GREG: Looks like it shouldn't cost too much to have all the carpet ripped up and replaced.

ALICE: I don't care how much it costs. I don't care about the carpet. Can we please just not say anything about it for a while? (*She reaches for another tissue, blows her nose, and sets the used tissue down on the table. ALICE eyes the book, but does not pick it up. As she speaks, she addresses GREG, though she doesn't look at him.*) How many subscribers?

GREG: Really?

ALICE: Yes, Greg. Please. I need a distraction.

GREG: Like 900K. Maybe a little over. I haven't checked today. The video's been trending for a few days. It's in the top three now.

ALICE: That's good, right?

GREG: Yeah. It just... doesn't feel the way I thought it would before.

ALICE: What about advertisers?

GREG: Everyone's come back, and then some. My inbox is full of sponsorship offers.

ALICE: That's good too, right?

GREG: Yeah.

ALICE: So tell your face that.

GREG: I don't know. I think... maybe it hasn't hit me yet. I'm only 100K shy of my goal, but it feels so far away. I feel so far away, from everything I've wanted. I feel like I understand so much less about myself than I did when I started this channel.

ALICE: You've changed a lot since then. We both have.

GREG: I almost wish we hadn't. (*ALICE toys with the collar. GREG closes the laptop and just watches her. She notices him staring.*) I almost wish the cops hadn't taken the boxes. I'm glad they're not here, and maybe the police can piece it all together, but I hate not really having anything to go on now.

ALICE: Should I have let them have the collar?

GREG: No. You were right to keep it. They checked it for fingerprints, but there weren't any. No traceable evidence... (*His voice trails off. He rubs the back of his neck.*) No more cameras, either. I followed them around while they were looking.

ALICE: I should have done that too. I just shut down. I'm sorry.

GREG: Don't worry about it. I wanted to do the same, but I just... I was too hopped up on adrenaline and riding the shock. If I didn't channel that, I might have punched a hole in the wall or something.

ALICE: I know you said you don't think it's anyone you know, but are there any other vloggers with a grudge against you? He knows your name, for God's sake.

GREG: Like rivals or something?

ALICE: Yeah, rivals, I guess. Anyone like that?

GREG: Not that I can think of. I go out of my way not to disparage anyone else's channels. It's like the one principle I still follow after all these years. (*He tries to crack a smirk, but it falls flat. He sighs.*) What about you? Make any enemies?

ALICE: Nope. (*Silence once again stretches between them. GREG shifts uncomfortably on the couch, not meeting ALICE's gaze as he speaks.*)

GREG: He threatened to take you away from me.

ALICE: What?

GREG: The Boxer. Along with... Rocco. He sent me an email too. I didn't want to tell you about it because it scared me shitless.

ALICE: It's too late not to scare me, Greg. I need to know what all we're up against here.

GREG: I know. That's why I... I need to tell you now. I need to tell you what he said, what he promised me would happen if I didn't offer him the "proper" tribute or whatever. The fucker.

ALICE: He told you he'd do something bad to me?

GREG: He told me he would take you, because I don't deserve you. Whatever the hell that means.

ALICE: We need to talk to the police again.

GREG: No. No police. He told me we couldn't, not anymore. *(He lowers his voice. As he speaks, his voice shakes.)* He's got eyes on the house. He said he would shoot you.

ALICE: Okay, fine. We won't go to the police. But... we should take precautions to make sure he can't make good on his threat somehow, right?

GREG: You shouldn't be here. You should go somewhere else. Somewhere safer. Lie low for a while, if you can.

ALICE: I can go to my mom's house. I'll leave in an hour.

GREG: I don't want you to go, but... I think it's for the best. As long as you're here, I can't protect you. I can't guarantee safety for either of us anymore. *(ALICE kisses him. She gets up from the couch, sets the collar on the table, and heads upstairs, presumably to pack her* *things. GREG puts his head in his hands. He fights the urge to cry. On the table, his cell phone rings. He stares at it for a minute before deciding to pick up.*) Hello? (*He listens for a moment, growing more and more distressed.*) I don't really feel like listening to you, but I don't have a choice anymore, is that right? (*On the other end of the line, the BOXER keeps talking. GREG gets up from the couch, goes over to his desktop computer, and boots it up. His hands tremble as he goes back to the couch, lifts up a cushion, and takes out a thumb drive, which he holds up and examines.*) And... if I do this, it will ruin my computer? But Alice will be safe, right? (*The BOXER hangs up. GREG lowers the phone from his ear. He looks at the computer for a long, long time before going over and putting in the thumb drive. Once it boots up, error codes and glitches display all over the computer monitors. Everything goes haywire, and then it goes black. Smoke pours out from behind the computer. GREG watches, defeated, although he understands that it is a necessary sacrifice. He has just started to relax when ALICE screams. Lights fade as he goes running up the stairs.*)

ACT II

Scene 4

(*Lights up on GREG and ALICE's bedroom, which is in shambles. Her open suitcase lies on the bed, with clothing and toiletries strewn everywhere. A lamp is upended. Drawers are thrown open in the dresser, and the bedroom window is broken. GREG's laptop sits on the bed, too. He paces as he talks on the phone.*)

GREG: I don't know what the fuck is wrong with you. I did everything right. I did everything you asked. I blew my fucking life up. You told me she'd be safe. You promised me — (*The BOXER, on the other end of the line, cuts him off.*) Yes, of course I do. More than anything. And if you hurt her, you sick son of a bitch, I swear, I'll — (*More words from the BOXER. GREG freezes.*) What? Why? I still have my laptop. I can pull it up right now, but... just tell me what you want, please. Tell me where to find her. (*The BOXER is quiet, and GREG looks at the phone in disbelief before going over to his laptop and booting it up.*) I'm doing it, okay? Just give me a minute. Please don't hang up. Please oh please. (*Per the BOXER's instructions, GREG pulls up his livestream video, one that has been uploaded on* his behalf. *He frowns at the screen.*) I thought all these got taken down. Serves me right, I guess. And you just want me to play it? The whole thing, I mean? (*On the other end of the phone, the BOXER says something else. GREG nods. He clicks play. The audio from the livestream starts, and once again, we hear GREG going into his spiel, before ROCCO starts barking, ALICE comes downstairs, and GREG and ALICE get into an argument. GREG winces as he listens to himself calling ALICE a bitch once again. He closes the laptop.*) I can't watch any more. Please. I wish I'd never made this. I treated her like shit. Please tell me I can stop. (*The BOXER says more on the other end of the line. GREG reluctantly opens the laptop and finishes watching the video. He pauses for a long time after it ends.*) Yeah, I exceeded my goal. One-point-two million subscribers. And no, I don't feel smug. I don't feel anything. (*Beat. The lights in the bedroom flicker. GREG drags a hand down his face.*) Can you please call your ghost off or whatever? Please. I've done everything you've asked me to so far. (*Another pause. The BOXER asks to be put on speaker phone.*) Yeah, okay. Hold on a second. (*GREG puts him on speaker phone. The BOXER's voice is distorted, as though conveyed through a voice disguiser, but it should still be easy for the audience to determine what is being said.*)

BOXER (V.O): Make sure the volume is turned up all the way, otherwise it won't work, Zipper.

GREG: Yeah, okay, I got it.

BOXER (V.O.): Hold the phone up.

GREG: Done.

BOXER (V.O.): Also, you'll want something sharp to cut your hand.

GREG: (*Scowling at the phone.*) Wait a minute, are you serious?

BOXER (V.O.): Blood to summon, blood to banish.

GREG: Jesus Christ. Okay. (*He opens his nightstand drawer and takes out something sharp. He presses the point against the palm of his hand that was injured before, applies pressure, and winces as he opens the cut back up. Blood drips off his palm and onto the floor.*)

BOXER (V.O.): Did you do it?

GREG: So, you really don't have cameras in here anymore.

BOXER (V.O.): Watch the attitude. I'll take that as a yes, though. Now then, let's get started. (*The BOXER clears his throat. With a great deal of ceremony, he recites the following incantation, with a similar rhyme scheme as before, meant to banish the ENTITY once and for all.*) Your mission has ended, you've witnessed the fool. Objective completed, submit to my rule. Now that it's over, the Entity leaves. Zipper, I have no more tricks up my sleeves. (*The lights in the house flicker violently, there is a demonic shriek, and another sonic boom. GREG fumbles the phone and drops it. Then, just as suddenly as it began, the house is back to normal. For the first time in a long time, GREG lets himself relax. He stoops to pick up the phone, still on speaker.*)

GREG: So, it's over then. The ghost is gone.

BOXER (V.O.): Gone, but far from forgotten, I hope.

GREG: I've learned my lesson, okay? I want Alice back now.

BOXER (V.O.): You think you deserve her?

GREG: No, I don't. I never have. But somehow, she still chose me. She chooses me every day, even when it's not easy. Even when I fuck it up. And I could spend the rest of my life trying to be worthy of her love and never make it. When I get her back... well, I want to try. I want to make it up to her in any way I can. Whatever she wants, I'll give her. I'm hers.

BOXER (V.O.): You know what she wants, more than anything in the world—your full, undivided attention. Are you prepared to give it to her, give up everything you hold so dear?

GREG: All of it and more.

BOXER (V.O.): Sounds like Greg is all grown up. But, I wonder... are you prepared to fight to save the one you love?

GREG: I'll do anything to get her back.

BOXER (V.O.): Including risking your own life? (*He lets the words hang in the air between them for a moment. GREG nods, then realizes that the BOXER can't see him.*)

GREG: Whatever it takes.

BOXER (V.O.): I'm sure she'll be glad to hear it. Meet me in Dover Park tonight, two o'clock in the morning. Come alone. You'll want to bring the gun as well. I detest an unfair fight. And... Greg.

GREG: Yes?

BOXER (V.O.): Record a video before. You know, just in case. (*The line goes dead with a click as he hangs up. GREG just stares at the phone for a moment before hanging up and setting up the* *video camera function on the phone. He points it at himself and begins to narrate.)*

GREG: Hey there, ghosts and ghouls. It's Greg. If you're watching this, it means I fucked up. Like, big time. And I failed to save the person I love most in this world. Don't wish me well, or hope I rest in peace. I won't. Now, I have to go put a few rounds in this fucker so he doesn't get the satisfaction of seeing this go live. *(GREG stops recording. He tucks the phone into his pocket, checks the clock that reads one a.m., and opens the nightstand drawer. Once again, he takes out the pistol, chambers a cartridge, and turns the safety off. He shoves the pistol into the waistband and heads out of the bedroom as the lights fade.)*

ACT II

Scene 5

(*Lights up on the park, the same one where GREG and ALICE had their date so long ago. GREG looks more uncomfortable than we have ever seen him, and for good reason: he's expecting the worst, and the BOXER hasn't given him any reason not to. He sits on the bench with a hand on the butt of his gun, scanning the park for any sight of his opponent. He shivers because the air is chilly. There is no sign of the BOXER. The only sounds for miles are wind and chirping crickets. GREG's cell phone rings, startling him. He answers it.*)

GREG: I'm here. Where are you? (*A woman screams on the other end of the line. It is loud enough for the audience to hear. GREG jumps up, still holding the phone.*) Alice, is that you? What's he doing? Are you hurt? (*Another scream. It dawns on GREG that this time, it's not coming from the phone. He hangs up and puts the phone back in his pocket, taking out the gun instead.*) Where the fuck are you? Show yourself! (*The sound of twigs cracking, branches breaking, leaves rustling. An owl hoots. GREG points the gun offstage, hands shaking as he does so. He doesn't look* *like he wants to fire it again, although he knows he might have to. At last, a figure steps out of the trees. This is the BOXER.)*

BOXER: Hello, Greg.

GREG: *(He turns the gun on the Boxer, hands still shaking.)* Fucker.

BOXER: Put the gun down, Greg. Let's both be civilized.

GREG: That went out the window when you murdered my dog.

BOXER: Alice's dog.

GREG: You son of a bitch. *(The owl hoots again, startling GREG so badly that he fumbles and drops the gun. He scrambles to pick it up. The BOXER remains calm. Seeing this, and realizing the BOXER is making no attempt to grab the gun himself, GREG slowly straightens up.)* You're not afraid of me.

BOXER: No.

GREG: I could kill you.

BOXER: Perhaps.

GREG: That still doesn't scare you? *(He reaches for the gun, hesitates, but the BOXER doesn't stop him. GREG stands.)*

BOXER: You don't want to kill me.

GREG: You have no idea.

BOXER: You won't want to kill me once you hear my proposition.

GREG: I'm sick of listening. Tell me, where's Alice? (*He cocks the hammer and points the gun at the BOXER.*) Tell me, God damn it.

BOXER: What if I could restore your channel, make it so your little livestream upload never happened?

GREG: (*He takes a step closer.*) I don't care about the channel.

BOXER: The channel is your life, Greg.

GREG: No. I thought it was. God, I wasted so much time pouring my heart out to virtual strangers, people who don't have my back and can't support me in my daily life. Through the real shit, like this. Alice is the only one. Alice is my life, not the fucking channel.

BOXER: Now you see. I just wanted you to see. (*He takes a step toward GREG, and GREG takes a step back.*) Are you going to shoot me?

GREG: I want to.

BOXER: I know.

GREG: But I want to see Alice.

BOXER: Of course. I'll take you to her. Please give me the gun. (*GREG hesitates again. Perhaps against his better judgment, he hands the gun off to the BOXER. The BOXER tucks it into the waistband of his pants, much to GREG's relief.*) You made the right choice.

GREG: If you say so. (*The BOXER kneels and starts running his hands over the ground, pulling at roots. GREG watches, confused,* *but also transfixed. At last, the BOXER uncovers a hatch and opens it. He and GREG peer into the hole. ALICE cries out.)*

ALICE: Greg!

BOXER: If you'd killed me, you never would have found her. She probably would have starved. (*The BOXER looks up, and his eyes meet GREG's. At that moment, it seems he knows what will happen next, but it is too late — GREG latches onto the BOXER and grapples with him. After a brief scuffle, the two men topple into the hole. We hear shouts, cursing, ALICE screaming — a gunshot. A keening wail. Then, silence. ALICE pulls herself out of the hole with a great deal of difficulty. She is disheveled, and blood is splattered on the side of her face and clothing. After a moment of collecting herself, she reaches a hand down to GREG. She pulls him up beside her. He's also covered in blood. He looks at ALICE, still in shock.*)

ALICE: Let's get out of here. (*Lights fade.*)

ACT II

Scene 6

(*Lights up on GREG and ALICE's basement, several days after the showdown. GREG has a black eye, but his hand is no longer bandaged. GREG has a new laptop, which is open on the couch beside him. He checks a few things and then goes live.*)

GREG: Hey there, ghosts and ghouls. You know who it is. I just wanted to thank you all for being so patient with me. When my channel went dark, so many rumors floated around. A lot of you thought had been arrested or killed or both. Many speculated I was quitting—and rightly so. (*He pauses.*) When I started this channel—well, when Alice helped me start this channel, I was just messing around. I was just a kid who liked ghosts and wanted to share spooky shit with the world. I never expected anything big to come from it. Now that I have one million subs... I don't feel like I expected to. I thought this would feel like winning the lottery, but it doesn't. No, what feels good to me—what *really* feels like winning the lottery—is shutting down this channel and focusing all my time on what matters most. On *who* matters most. And, if I'm lucky, spending the rest of my life with her. Having kids with her, even. Can you keep a secret? (*He takes out a black box, opens it, and shows the ring to the camera.*) I've been to so many haunted locations, encountered so many weird, unexplained phenomena… but nothing terrifies me like what I'm about to do. And, at the same time, I've never been so certain. So, wish me luck, will you? And… this is me, signing off. (*He snaps the box closed, puts his hand on the laptop. He hesitates. Although he knows he's made the right choice, it doesn't come easy. Then, he closes his eyes, sighs, and closes the laptop. He gets up from the couch, puts the ring in his pocket, and heads up the stairs. Blackout. End of play.*)

Acknowledgments

This book would not exist without my Patreon supporters. Your generosity makes it possible to do more of what I love, and for that, I am eternally grateful. In particular, thanks to Author Ivy James, Avalon Roselin, Bri Leclerc, Cameron Evesque Davis, Cassie Kelley, Chris Mahan, Emma Fink, Harley Green, J. P. Dailing, Jax Wells, Jinne Noble, Kate Mitchell, Katie Reitzel, Kay Adams, Mary-Keith Vorasingha, Tom Peck, Valerie Rutherford, and WheresMyPen. I love you all so much.

Also, to my Kickstarter backers, you mean the world to me. From the bottom of my heart, thank you to the following supporters: Emma Fink, Carrie Conway, Michelle Carl, Rachel, Guest 1832980333, The Creative Fund by BackerKit, Elizabeth, Angelicide, Brian Morgan, Joseph Malesky, Scott, Jennifer Acres, Bri Ollre, Hollie Satterfield, Jillian, Neal, Laura Hurtig, Kimberly Wix, Colin, Holly Jender, Jorge Haro, Arioch Morningstar, Kate Harvie, Eric D. Walters, Vince Rostkowski, and Dominique Bowens. I sincerely couldn't have published this play without you.

Additional thanks to Johannus M. Steger for this excellent cover, and Gemma Amor for the heartfelt blurb. This book would not look this professional without you. Thank you, thank you, thank you.

About the Author

Briana Morgan is a horror and fantasy author, playwright, freelance editor, and writing consultant. Her books include *Livingston Girls*, *A Writer's Guide to Slaying Social*, *Reflections*, *Touch: A One-Act Play*, and *Blood and Water*. In addition to writing, she's also active on social media, especially on Instagram (@brianamorganbooks) and Twitter (@brimorganbooks).

Briana lives with her partner and two cats in Atlanta.

Also by Briana Morgan

Livingston Girls

A Writer's Guide to Slaying Social

Reflections

Touch: A One-Act Play

Blood and Water